Flemming in God's Armor

JANICE DEAN
SUSAN HENSON
PAM MASHBURN
KIMBERLY SHEPPARD

illustrated by
KAREN CRAFT

ISBN-10: 1480036137
ISBN-13: 9781480036130

This book belongs to......

The Flemming Adventures......
Flemming in God's Armor

Thanks to our families and friends for their support and encouragement along the journey. Karen Craft...you did it again! You are awesome. You were able to take the words and make them come to life. You knew what we wanted even when we didn't. Thanks for using the talent God has given you. Bro. Al, you are a great cheerleader—many thanks. We appreciate your support. Linda Dunsmore, thanks for the time you took to edit our many versions.

Fred Rainer, your technical expertise sealed the deal.

FORWARD

In this story of Flemming the snake, he reminds us that God doesn't care about our outward appearance. Instead, God is more concerned about our heart. Flemming is introduced to a group of animals who teach him an important lesson through God's word, by explaining how we need to put on God's armor everyday. As you read this book to your children, I pray that your family will grow closer to God with the help of this little snake. I am looking forward to Flemming's next adventure.
Barry Saunders, Children's Pastor, Bethany Baptist Church
John 10:10

Dedicated to the Memory of Crystal Kirkland Clark
July 23, 1984 – December 23, 2010

This book is dedicated in memory of Crystal Kirkland Clark. The character, Kimberly, is a lot like Crystal, very friendly and always ready to help people. Children and animals were the core of her heart. She always had a wonderful smile that would warm your heart, now she is smiling with Jesus forever!

When Flemming arrived home from the mission trip to Canada, he was so excited. He had a new best friend—Jesus!

He couldn't wait to go to Sunday school and church with his new friends from the mission team he met in Canada. When he went to church on Sunday, Kimberly was the first to greet him and invited him to her Sunday School class. There he learned about baptism. The teacher explained that it meant he had a new life and was going to follow Jesus. The teacher said, "Flemming, if you would like, you can be baptized today!" "Yippee!" cried Flemming! He could hardly wait! He wasn't a mean, hissing snake anymore and that made him smile.

As the pastor baptized him, all of his friends from the mission team and other new friends were there to celebrate with him. He had friends for the very first time, but his best friend is Jesus. When he came out of the water everyone clapped because they were so proud that he was not afraid to show how much he loved Jesus.

When it was time for the pastor to talk, he spoke about the importance of obeying God's Word. Flemming thought, "I am learning so much." Next week, the pastor said, "I will tell about God's armor from Ephesians 6 in the Bible." "That's cool," thought Flemming. He just knew that he would look strong and handsome in a suit of armor. He was going to ask Kimberly how to get one. Kimberly always answered his questions. She is a good friend.

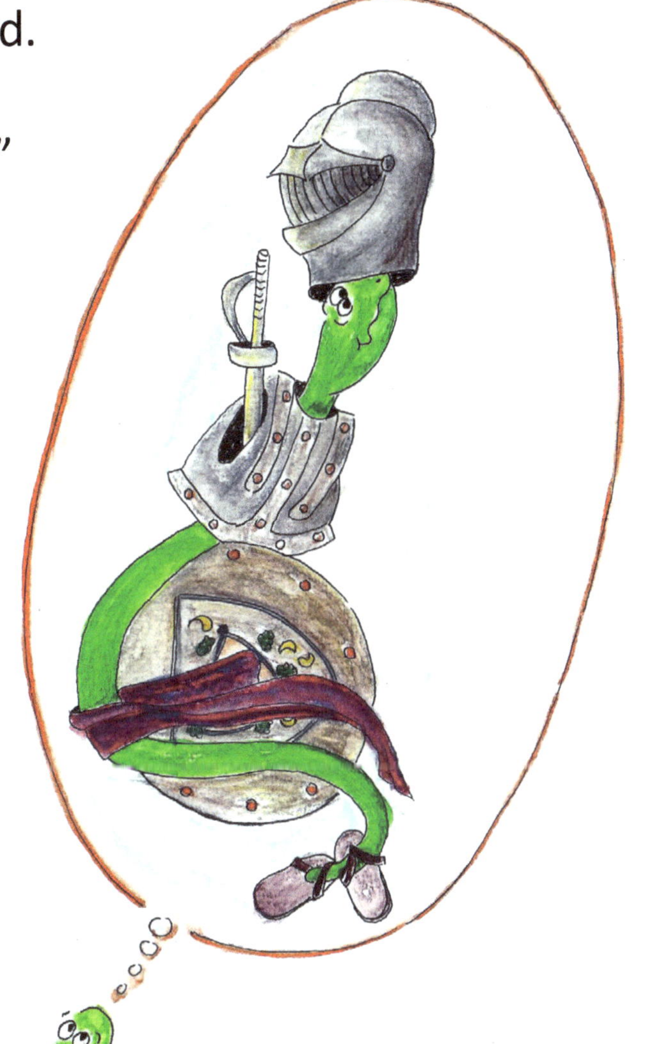

After church, Flemming asked Kimberly, "What does the pastor mean about following Jesus everyday and putting on the full armor?" Kimberly said, "Flemming, we need to put on the full armor of God to protect us from the devil's tricks. The devil wants us to mess up and do things God doesn't want us to do," Kimberly explained. "He tries to get us interested in violent video games, shows on TV or movies that we shouldn't watch, or to disobey our parents. When we put on the armor of God, we will be able to stand up to these things and do what is right. The devil is sneaky. You don't have to be afraid of him, but you have to be ready to fight him. He will use every trick to get you to turn away from God. The armor will give you God's help to fight against the devil," said Kimberly.

"This was so exciting," Flemming thought. He tried to imagine how he was going to get into that suit of armor. Flemming knew that Jesus would help him put on the armor. He just had to find one.

That afternoon,
our friend
Flemming
decided to go
for a slither
in the woods
near his home.
He was getting
ready to be
on another
adventure and
he didn't even
know it. As he slithered through the woods,
admiring God's creation, he heard singing
coming from just up ahead in the clearing. He
stopped, moved his little green head to one side
and listened.....

Armor's going on,
Armor's going on
Helmet on my head.
Helmet on my head.
It protects what I think and say.
God watches out for me everyday.
I have my helmet on.
I have my helmet on.

Flemming thought to himself, "I haven't heard that song before, but I sure do like it. But, who in the world is singing? Usually the woods are so quiet, but not today!"

Flemming slithered slowly into the clearing. When he looked up, he saw a group of animals— a snake wearing glasses, a bright green turtle, a masked raccoon, a colorful peacock, a wise old owl and a courageous squirrel.

"Ahem, excuse me, my name is Flemming,"
he hissed. "I heard your song, but what does
it mean?"

The snake slithered up to Flemming, pushed his
glasses up with his tongue and said, "Hello, I am
Jake the Snake and we're practicing for a play at
church about the Full Armor of God."

"Oh, I learned about that at church yesterday,"
replied Flemming. "But, I don't understand it at
all. Why do we need to wear the armor of
God every day?"

"Well, well little friend, we'll start at the top of our head and work our way down so we can remember each piece of armor to put on. First is the **Helmet of Salvation**. We use the helmet to protect our minds.

Always remember that we're God's children and He loves us and will help us.
We also need to remember what we've read in the Bible and learned from our parents and church about God. That will help us make the right decisions. Do you understand so far?" asked Jake. "Yes," hissed Flemming. "Next, you put on the **Breastplate of Righteousness,"** said Jake, **"**but, I'm going to let Ricky the Raccoon tell you about it. He's an expert!"

Ricky crept slowly up to Flemming. "Hello," he said, "I'm Ricky the Raccoon, and Jake is right. You need to know why it's important to wear the **Breastplate of Righteousness.** It protects the part between our neck and tummy. And, it also protects our heart," said Ricky. "We can protect our heart by telling God about the things we've done wrong. Flemming, always do what is right and good. That way, the devil can't sneak into your heart," he warned.

Then Ricky asked, "Where is Earl the Squirrel? It's his turn to tell Flemming about the **Belt of Truth**. He's always wandering off looking for nuts." Ricky cleared his throat and said in a LOUD voice, "Earl, Earl, where are you?" Just then, Earl came scampering down a tree with his mouth full of nuts. Flemming noticed Earl had a belt around his waist. He was quite a sight! "Earl," said Ricky, "Pay attention. Tell Flemming about the **Belt of Truth**. And, don't talk with your mouth full." "CHOMP, CHOMP, CHOMP," went Earl trying to eat the nuts he had gathered. "Well," (gulp) Earl the Squirrel swallowed the nuts and began to explain. "You need to know the truth about God and you can learn it by reading the Bible every day. John 17:17 tells us that God's Word is truth. So, when you wear the Belt it will help you to always tell the truth...to your parents, your teachers and friends. We need to always tell the truth."

Flemming heard a commotion. All of the animals were talking at once. Flemming looked up and saw a peacock strutting

toward him, spreading her colorful feathers. She was beautiful! Flemming had never seen anything like her before. "Hello, Flemming. I'm Priscilla the Peacock, but you can call me Prissy. It's nice to meet you. Do you like my sandals? They're the **Sandals of Peace**. I just love them. Don't they look cute? It is important to put them on every day before you go out." Now this really confused Flemming. He didn't have feet. How could he wear sandals? He would remember to ask Kimberly. She would know.

"Flemming, Flemming, are you listening to me?" Prissy asked. "Yes, Prissy, I'm listening," Flemming replied. "We need to protect our feet and go where God would want us to go. Our feet should be ready to take us to tell others the good news about Jesus," said Prissy.

The next piece of armor is the **Shield of Faith**, but WHO would tell Flemming about the Shield?

Suddenly, Flemming heard a loud noise....HOOT, HOOT, HOOT. He stretched his long scaly neck and looked up. Perched high on a branch in an old oak tree sat Ollie, the wise old owl. Ollie flapped his wings and blinked his eyes several times. "Is he ever going to talk to me?" thought Flemming. Ollie cleared his throat, "Ahem, hello young man. So you want to know about the **Shield of Faith**?" "Yes, I do," Flemming replied. "Just think of what you could do with a real shield," said Ollie. "If someone throws a rock at you, you can lift the shield so it doesn't hit you at all. We can use the shield in the same way when we're tempted to do things that will get us in trouble. We need to hold up our shield and stop these thoughts when this happens and remember that God loves us no matter what. God is our shield."

When Ollie finished explaining to Flemming about the **Shield of Faith**, he looked around. "Myrtle, quit hiding behind that bush and come here and tell Flemming about the **Sword of the Spirit,**" said Ollie. Myrtle the Turtle peeked out from behind the bush and shyly crept toward Flemming. "Speak up," said Ollie, "Don't be shy. Tell our little friend, Flemming, why he needs the **Sword of the Spirit."** "Hello Flemming," said Myrtle the Turtle. "I guess you know by now that I'm Myrtle the Turtle. The **Sword of the Spirit** is my favorite. The Sword is the Bible. By knowing God's Word, the Bible, we will be able to tell what is good and what is bad."

This gave Flemming a lot to think about. He decided that he needed to try and find these things that his new friends told him about. He told his new friends that he would see them again soon and he left to go shopping.

PRODUCE
ARMOR SHOP
ARMOR SHOP

Flemming started shopping for the armor of God, buying one piece each day.

On **Monday**, Flemming bought a helmet. Boy, did that give him a headache!

On **Tuesday**, he bought a breastplate. Wearing it made it very hard to breathe.

On **Wednesday**, he bought a belt, but it kept slipping off.

On **Thursday**, he bought sandals even though he had no feet to put them on.

On **Friday**, he bought a shield. He liked to coil up behind it and hide.

On **Saturday**, he bought a sword, but since he was a snake, he wasn't going to be able to carry it.

Flemming now had all of the pieces of armor. "How would he ever get dressed by himself each day?" he thought. It was so heavy. Flemming rolled over and over as he tried to put on each piece. When he stopped rolling, he was so tired he couldn't move. "How will I ever be able to tell people about Jesus if I have to wear this armor every day?" Flemming wondered. "I have to take this off and talk with Kimberly tomorrow at church." So, he rolled and rolled and rolled. Each time he rolled over, a piece of the armor came off. He remembered what Jake the Snake said about nothing being too big or too impossible with God.   He decided to pray to Jesus before he went to bed.

"Jesus, please help me to be able to wear your armor every day. I can't do this by myself," prayed Flemming.

When Kimberly saw Flemming on the way to church on Sunday, she could barely see his face. He was quite a sight! Kimberly laughed to herself as she had never seen anything like this before.

Flemming explained to Kimberly, "I bought a suit of armor just like the pastor and my friends in the forest told me to do, but it is too heavy to wear each day. How will I ever be protected from the devil's tricks?" asked Flemming.

Kimberly explained, "There is a story in the Bible about King David when he was a young boy and how he couldn't wear armor to fight the giant Goliath. He couldn't wear it because it was too heavy. He prayed for God to protect him from the evil Giant Goliath. God gave him the help he needed." Flemming sighed, "Well, if he couldn't wear it, how do you expect me to wear it?"

Kimberly laughed, "Oh Flemming, I didn't mean a **real** suit of armor. God's armor is invisible, and the only way the armor will work is if Jesus lives in your heart. When you get up every morning, you pray and imagine you are putting on the armor of God. Prayer holds all our armor together. You wear the armor to protect yourself against the devil."

"So Flemming, be sure to remember this very special piece of the armor...prayer. By talking to God we can do unbelievable things. Nothing is too big or impossible with prayer because God can do anything. That doesn't mean he will always answer our prayers the way we want, but he will always answer the way He knows is best for us. Remember when we were on the mission trip in Canada, what Roy the Magpie taught you about prayer?" asked Kimberly. "Yes," Flemming replied, "I do. God answered Roy's prayers. I found my way when I was lost and I found my new best friend....Jesus."

"That's right, Flemming," said Kimberly. "Why don't you come with me. We have a special group who is going to perform a play. I think the play will help you to better understand the armor of God."

Kimberly and Flemming found a seat on the
front row. Flemming could hardly
wait to see the play.

But, wait...look! It's the animals from the forest!
There was Jake the Snake, Myrtle the Turtle,
Ricky Raccoon, Prissy Peacock, Ollie Owl, and
Earl the Squirrel. As the music started, he
thought to himself, "That's the music I heard
in the forest. This play is going to be about the
armor of God." All of the animals began to sing.

When the play was over, Flemming exclaimed, "Finally, I understand what everyone has been trying to explain to me! Now every day the first thing I will do after I wake up is pray, and I will imagine putting on the full armor of God when I pray," hissed Flemming. "I'm ready for my next adventure!"

Where in the world will Flemming go next?

The Armor of God Song
To the tune of Three Blind Mice

(Put your hands on your head)
Armor's going on,
Armor's going on
Helmet on my head.
Helmet on my head.
It protects what I think and say.
God watches out for me everyday.
I have my helmet on.
I have my helmet on.

(Make a heart with your hands on your chest)
Armor's going on,
Armor's going on
Breastplate on my chest.
Breastplate on my chest.
It protects my heart each day.
I tell God I'm sorry when I pray.
I have my breastplate on.
I have my breastplate on.

(Pretend like you are putting on a belt)
Armor's going on,
Armor's going on,
Belt is on my waist.
Belt is on my waist.

My Bible tells me all the truth.
That way I know just what to do.
I have my belt on.
I have my belt on.

(Bend over and pretend like
you are putting on shoes)
Armor's going on,
Armor's going on,
Sandals on my feet.
Sandals on my feet.
God will lead us where to go.
Avoid the places we shouldn't go.
I have my sandals on.
I have my sandals on.

(Hold up one hand with your fingers out)
Armor's going on,
Armor's going on,
Shield is in my hand.
Shield is in my hand.
It bounces all the bad things off.
It keeps the devil from messing with me.
I have my shield with me.
I have my shield with me.

*(Hold up your other hand in a fist like you are
holding a sword)*
Armor's going on,
Armor's going on,
Sword is in my hand.
Sword is in my hand.
My sword is my Bible that tells me.
What is good and bad, you will see.
I have my sword with me.
I have my sword with me.

(Put your hands together like you are praying)

Armor's going on,
Armor's going on,
Prayer is covering me.
Prayer is covering me.
Prayer is talking to God each day.
It holds all my armor together to stay.
Prayer is covering me.
Prayer is covering me.